W9-BNS-589

After HAPPILY —EVER— AFTER.

The Frog Prince
Hops to It

After Happily Ever After was published in the United States
in 2009 and 2014 by Stone Arch Books, A Capstone Imprint
1710 Roe Crest Drive, North Mankato, Minnesota 56003
www.capstoneyoungreaders.com

First published by Orchard Books, a division of Hachette Children's Books
338 Euston Road, London NW1 3BH, United Kingdom

Text copyright © Tony Bradman, 2006
Illustrations copyright © Sarah Warburton, 2006
The right of Tony Bradman to be identified as the author and Sarah
Warburton as the illustrator of this Work has been asserted by them
in accordance with the Copyright Designs and Patents Act 1988.

All rights reserved. No part of this publication may be reproduced in
whole or in part, or stored in a retrieval system, or transmitted in any
form or by any means, electronic, mechanical, photocopying, recording,
or otherwise, without written permission of the publisher.

Library of Congress Cataloging-in-Publication Data is available
on the Library of Congress website.

ISBN: 978-1-4342-7962-0 (paperback)

Summary: Prince Freddy is no longer a frog, but he misses the big pond.
However, Princess Daisy thinks the pond is muddy, smelly, and gross.
Prince Freddy must make his wife understand how amazing the pond is
before it's too late.

Designer: Russell Griesmer
Photo Credits: ShutterStock/Maaike Boot, 5, 6, 7, 52, 53

Printed in China.
092013   007737LEOS14

After HAPPILY -EVER- AFTER

The Frog Prince
Hops to It

by TONY BRADMAN

illustrated by SARAH WARBURTON

STONE ARCH BOOKS®
a capstone imprint

TABLE OF CONTENTS

So Freddy turned back into
a prince, married Daisy,
and lived happily ever after.
And then ...

CHAPTER ONE

Prince Freddy quietly opened the back door of the royal mansion and slipped inside. He tiptoed down the hall.

He stopped at a door to make sure there was no one around. Then he dashed across the hall.

Whew, I made it! he thought as he began
to climb the stairs. But suddenly a shadow
fell across him.

He looked up and gulped. His lovely wife, Princess Daisy, was scowling down at him from the landing.

"So you finally came home," she said.

"Listen, darling," said Prince Freddy. "I can explain, honest."

"Don't bother," Daisy said. "I know where you've been. You're covered in mud and you smell gross. When are you going to realize that you're not a frog anymore, Freddy?"

Freddy sighed. He had been a frog for a long time. Actually, he had been a prince who had been transformed into a frog by the Wicked Witch.

He had lived at the big pond, but then he met Daisy at a local well.

Eventually she had freed him from the curse with a kiss, and they were married. At first, they had been blissfully happy.

But now it seemed they didn't really have much in common. Daisy had become interested in doing charity work, and she was always busy.

She was always getting involved in
campaigns for good causes, such as
the Fading Fairy Fund, the Hansel and
Gretel Kids in Trouble Helpline, even the
Keep the Forest Clean and Green Club.

Freddy wasn't exactly sure what he liked doing now that he was a person again. He had really enjoyed being a frog, and he missed it. He missed the pond and his froggy friends too.

"I know I'm not a frog anymore,"
Freddy said. "I just like spending time
down at the big pond, that's all. What's
wrong with that?"

"Nothing, I suppose," Daisy said. "Not if you think hanging around a smelly old pond is a good idea. But I don't. I think it's silly. I wish you could find something more serious to do. Now if you'll excuse me, I have some important letters to write."

And with that, Daisy turned on her heel and stomped off to her office.

CHAPTER TWO

Freddy trudged upstairs to their bedroom. He knew that Daisy didn't like him going to the big pond. That was why he kept sneaking there in secret.

But that obviously hadn't worked.
And he hated tricking her. It just didn't
feel right.

Freddy decided to take a bath. As he relaxed in the water, he wondered what to do. He loved Daisy, and he thought she still loved him. But he loved the big pond too. If only Daisy felt the same way about it.

He was sure she would if she understood
how amazing it was. So why didn't he
show her?

"Yes, that's it!" he said, and leaped
out of the bath.

He threw on some clothes and sat
down at his desk.

Then he glanced at the calendar on the wall. Daisy's birthday was coming up in a few weeks. *Even better!* he thought, and he started making plans.

CHAPTER THREE

The morning of Daisy's birthday
arrived. When she woke up, Freddy
gave her a huge birthday card.

Then he led her down to the royal
dining room, where there was an
enormous pile of presents.

"Are these all for me?" said Daisy. "You shouldn't have, Freddy."

She gave him a lovely smile, the kind he hadn't seen for a while.

"Well, aren't you going to open them?" said Freddy, smiling back.

Daisy picked up a present and quickly ripped off the wrapping paper.

"Oh, it's a book," she said, her smile fading. "About ponds."

"Yes, and it's got some really great pictures in it," Freddy said.

There were more books too, including
Fairy Tale Ponds, *Life On A Lily Pad*, and
Time for Slime.

There were DVDs about ponds, a pond poster, a special Pond-Watcher's Kit, and even a pair of slippers shaped like frogs.

Daisy's smile vanished, and her bottom lip quivered.

"Well," said Freddy, thinking that he might have made a mistake. "I was planning to take you for a lovely picnic at the big pond."

"I don't believe it!" Daisy wailed. "This is the worst birthday I've ever had. I'm beginning to wonder why I married you in the first place. You're going to have to make your mind up, Freddy! It's that pond or me!"

Then she burst into tears and ran out.
Freddy followed and tried to talk to her,
but she locked herself in her office and
refused to see him.

CHAPTER FOUR

That afternoon, Freddy trudged off to say a final good-bye to the big pond. He had made his choice, but he still felt sad.

He stood by the cool, green water.
He listened to the insects buzzing and
the soft, plopping sounds as his froggy
friends dived in. Then he heard another
sound — a banging.

A man was putting up a sign nearby.
Freddy read the sign and felt very uneasy.

ADVANCE NOTICE
OF
DEVELOPMENT

"Hi," Freddy said. "Would you mind telling me what that sign means?"

"Sure," said the man. "We're putting an eight-lane highway through here soon. We start draining the pond tomorrow."

Freddy was horrified. "You can't do that!" he said. "What's going to happen to all the creatures who live in it?"

"Not my problem," said the man, and walked off. "Goodbye!"

Freddy was angry now. Even if he never
went to the big pond again, he just had to
save it and his friends! But how? Then an
idea came to him, and he smiled.

He couldn't do it on his own. He needed a big campaign, and he knew just the person to help him get it organized. Freddy ran home as fast as he could.

CHAPTER FIVE

Soon he was standing outside Daisy's office door again. He raised his hand to knock, but then he stopped. What if Daisy didn't want to be involved?

But somehow Freddy had a feeling
that she would, as long as he could
persuade her to talk to him. She opened
her door as soon as she heard him say
the words "good cause."

"An eight-lane highway!" she said, just
as upset as Freddy. "Of course I'll help.
It might only be a smelly old pond, but
destroying it would be a total disaster for
the forest!"

"Now let me see. We'll have to make some posters, put together a petition, and organize a demonstration," she said. And that was how the Save the Big Pond campaign was born.

Daisy threw herself into it with all her energy. She read the books Freddy had given her and was amazed at how many different types of frogs there were.

That would be useful for the posters, she thought.

She watched the DVDs too, and they gave her the idea for Wet Rock: The Concert to Save the Big Pond.

She even went to the big pond with
Freddy, where her special pond-watcher's
kit came in handy. (Although she never did
wear the slippers shaped like frogs.)

The campaign was a huge success, and the big pond was saved forever. Freddy was delighted, but he also realized that he had really loved working on it. So he asked Daisy if he could help with her other good causes too.

He took everything very seriously,
and worked just as hard as Daisy. They
became a terrific, unbeatable team.
(Although they made sure they always
had plenty of fun as well.)

So Daisy and Freddy and their froggy
friends really did live happily ever after.

ABOUT THE AUTHOR

Tony Bradman writes for children of all ages. He is particularly well known for his top-selling Dilly the Dinosaur series. His other titles include the Happily Ever After series, *The Orchard Book of Heroes and Villains*, and *The Orchard Book of Swords, Sorcerers*, and *Superheroes*. Tony lives in South East London.

ABOUT THE ILLUSTRATOR

Sarah Warburton is a rising star in children's books. She is the llustrator of the Rumblewick series, which has been very well received at an international level. The series spans across both picture books and fiction. She has also illustrated nonfiction titles and the Happily Ever After series. She lives in Bristol, England, with her young baby and husband.